SIR GADABOUT
Goes Overboard

SIR GADABOUT
Goes Overboard

Martyn Beardsley
Illustrated by Tony Ross

Dolphin Paperbacks

First published in Great Britain in 2004
as a Dolphin Paperback
by Orion Children's Books
a division of the Orion Publishing Group Ltd
Orion House
5 Upper St Martin's Lane
London   WC2H 9EA

A catalogue record for this book is
available from the British Library

Printed in Great Britain by
Clays Ltd, St Ives plc

ISBN   1 84255 274 0

For Sarah in the Windy City

Contents

1   Sir Gadabout Digs a Hole   1

2   Anchors Aweigh!   13

3   Longbeard's Long-Gone Beard   23

4   Little Jim has a Quiet Word   33

5   Sir Gadabout to the Rescue   39

6   Well, Sort of . . .   45

7   Sir Gadabout Runs Away   49

8   The Final Showdown   53

9   Sir Gadabout Walks the Plank   63

10   Sir Gadabout Pulls the Plug   73

1

Sir Gadabout Digs a Hole

A long, long time ago, before even the first Harry Potter book was made into a film, there was a marvellous castle with wondrous towers and flags of every colour fluttering in the gentle summer breeze. The castle was surrounded by a moat and had high and mighty walls designed to keep out even the most powerful of enemies. That was all very well – until the whole thing was accidentally flattened by a donkey called Elvis who was carrying children along the beach for £1.50 a go.

"It's happened *again*!" cried Herbert, throwing his bucket and spade down in disgust as he surveyed the shapeless pile of sand with flags sticking out of it. Herbert was a squire – the helper of a knight in armour in the far-off days before the first Harry Potter film.

The knight who Herbert was squire to dropped his own bucket and spade – bringing a halt to work on his tunnel to Australia – and marched over to the Donkey Man. "My dear

sir," he complained, "don't you think you ought to have a proper donkey path for your animals?"

"Don't you think you ought to mind your own business and get back in that hole where you belong?" replied the Donkey Man rather rudely.

"Now look here, I am a Knight of the Round Table, and let me tell you —"

"I know who you are, mate," interrupted the Donkey Man. "You're the Worst Knight in the World. *The Silliest Sausage to Carry a Sword* it said in the papers the other day, after you were chased all the way back to Camelot by that little piggy!"

"*Little* piggy, you say?" said Sir Gadabout (for indeed it was he). "It was big and ugly, with a ferocious *oink* like a – a – *wolf*!"

"Wolves don't go *oink*," the Donkey Man pointed out knowledgeably. "Not even ferociously."

"Well *I've* heard one!" Herbert said, sticking up for his master as he always did. "Woke me up in the middle of the night! Oinking ferociously – somewhere near the Camelot pigsty. I *think* it was a wolf, anyway . . ."

Just then, Sidney Smith came back with the

ice-creams. He was a cat belonging to Merlin the mysterious wizard. Sidney Smith was rather grumpy; he only seemed to cheer up when making cruel jokes at Sir Gadabout's expense.

Seeing the argument taking place between Sir Gadabout and the Donkey Man, Sidney Smith decided to have a little fun. "Don't meddle with that knight – he'd make short work of you, mate!"

"Oh, *would* he?" said the Donkey Man, rolling up his sleeves.

"Now, now, Sidney," warned Sir Gadabout.

"You wouldn't stand a chance against a great knight like *him*!" the cat continued.

"Him and whose army? That's what I'd like to know," declared the Donkey Man, removing his spectacles.

"*Stop it!*" commanded Sir Gadabout nervously.

"Right!" said Sidney Smith, passing the ice-creams to Herbert. "I'm going to fetch his sword!" And with that he marched away in a determined fashion. Herbert had a lick of all three ice-creams (well, he *had* to – they were starting to dribble).

"Sword?" screamed the Donkey Man, suddenly looking far less brave. "HELP! MURDER! HE'S GOT A BIG SWORD AND HE'S GONE MAD!"

Before long, an angry crowd had surrounded Sir Gadabout, shouting and waving their fists. The children on the donkeys were crying and the donkeys were making that sound they make (I would tell you what it was but I don't know how to spell it). Sidney Smith was watching from the top of the Punch and Judy tent, trimming his claws with the sword and chuckling quietly to himself. Herbert was working hard to make sure the ice-creams didn't dribble.

"*He's murdered the Donkey Man!*" cried someone from the crowd.

"That's what he did, all right!" agreed the Donkey Man.

"*And what about the kiddies?*" screamed a woman waving her knitting needles about in a dangerous manner. "*Fancy murdering poor little children before they've even done anything wrong!*"

"*I bet he's even murdered a DONKEY!*" yelled the ice-cream seller, waving a 99 around (but not very dangerously). "*LET'S GET HIM!*"

The crowd was actually not surrounding Sir Gadabout so much as the hole that he'd jumped into. Herbert had by now finished the ice-creams and was bravely standing guard by the hole, jabbing a Welsh flag on a little stick at anyone who dared get too close.

There was the sound of frantic digging and clouds of sand were flying wildly into the air.

"I didn't kill any*one* or any*thing*!" protested Sir Gadabout's echoey voice. He hoped he was at least as far as Sierra Leone by now (even though he wasn't sure exactly where it was).

"There was that crab, sire . . ." Herbert mentioned helpfully.

"But – but – it was hidden in the sand

where I was digging!" Sir Gadabout spluttered. The mob wasn't impressed.

"*Animal killer!*"

"*Call the animal welfare people!*"

Their fury grew and grew, until suddenly, something happened that made everyone forget about Sir Gadabout (much to Sidney Smith's disappointment).

Loud bangs like thunderclaps boomed out at sea. Two sailing ships wreathed in smoke

appeared to be doing battle. Everyone ran to the shoreline to watch.

"Throw me a rope, Herbert, or I'll never be able to get out of this hole!" called Sir Gadabout urgently.

"But, sire, the top of your head is still sticking out of the top of the hole . . ."

Sir Gadabout looked up – in fact, he *stood* up, for he had been kneeling down to dig – and discovered that the hole only came up to just above his knees. "Very well – I shall attempt to climb out," he said, with as much dignity as he could muster.

"It's Captain Hazard of the *Flying Barnacle*," said the ice-cream man worriedly as he watched the sea battle. "He's being attacked by Longbeard the pirate!"

"Longbeard will be the ruin of us!" wailed the Donkey Man.

"What's all this about?" asked Sir Gadabout, greatly relieved that someone other than him was going to be the ruin of them for a change.

"Everyone is leaving town because of that pesky pirate," the Donkey Man explained. "Most people here rely on doing business by sea, but Longbeard is making it so dangerous that hardly anyone dares set sail any more!"

"Why don't *you* do something about it?" the ice-cream seller asked Sir Gadabout. "You're a knight."

"He's a knight in *armour* – not in a life-jacket," scoffed Sidney Smith.

But the idea of defeating a wicked pirate captured Sir Gadabout's imagination. He had never been to sea before. "We Knights of the Round Table are supposed to help *anyone* in distress," he said proudly. "Ahoy there! Gather up our stuff, Herbert! Lead me to my ship!"

"I get seasick . . ." said Herbert, already looking a little green.

"You won't worry about that when you're *drowning*," groaned Sidney Smith.

2
Anchors Aweigh!

The crowd on the beach made its way to the harbour to witness the return of the *Flying Barnacle*.

"Oh dear," Sir Gadabout observed. "It's broken!"

"You would be too if the *Nasty Piece of Work* had fired a broadside at you," Sidney Smith pointed out. Then, seeing Sir Gadabout's blank expression, he explained, "A broadside is when all of the cannons down one side of a ship fire at you at once."

And indeed, the *Flying Barnacle* was in a sorry state. Her masts were splintered and smashed and most of her sails were in tatters.

While the ship was being repaired, the Donkey Man led the crowd over to see Captain Hazard. He was looking miserable.

"That Longbeard has nearly ruined me! One more attack like that and I won't be able to afford to go to sea again. What can I do? If I set sail he'll steal all my cargo; if I stay here the stuff is useless anyway."

"I have the answer," declared the Donkey Man. "A bold knight of the Round Table!" He pointed at Sir Gadabout.

"Hurray!" cheered the crowd.

"I recognise him . . ." said Captain Hazard. Sir Gadabout puffed his chest out proudly.

". . . he was chased by that little piggy."

Sir Gadabout let his chest go back in again

and mumbled something about 'ferocious oink'.

"What can *he* do against Longbeard, the most feared pirate on the seven seas?"

"Err . . ." began the Donkey Man.

"Err . . ." began the crowd.

"He killed a crab single-handedly . . ." ventured the ice-cream man.

But it was Herbert who saved the day. He boldly stepped forward with his master's sword, lance and shield. "Sir Gadabout is a brave warrior! He has been in countless fights against all kinds of terrifying enemies!" Herbert thought it best not to mention that Sir Gadabout had lost all his fights against terrifying enemies (and enemies who weren't very terrifying at all).

"Hurray!" cheered the crowd again.

Captain Hazard sighed. "I don't suppose I've got much choice . . ."

The repairs to the *Flying Barnacle* were

completed the following day and Sir Gadabout, Herbert and Sidney Smith watched as all that was left of Captain Hazard's cargo was loaded back on board.

Captain Hazard traded in wool. He bought it from the local sheep farmers and took it all the way to the Chilliwilli islands, where the sheep had no wool of their own and went around shivering and goose-pimply. Wool was worth almost as much as gold there, where they knitted it into coats for the poor sheep. Captain Hazard's problem was that Longbeard kept stealing his wool and all the money from it himself.

"If I don't sell that lot," the captain said to Sir Gadabout, "I'm finished. I need the money from selling the wool to pay my men,

for the upkeep of my ship – and to buy my *next* lot of wool."

"Never fear!" Sir Gadabout reassured him. "I have never lost a battle at sea yet!"

"Only because you've never been to sea," said Sidney Smith.

Once they were on board, Sir Gadabout became so excited that he couldn't stop himself from shouting commands like, "*Lower the mainbrace!*" and "*All hands to the starboard thingymijiggles!*" Consequently, confused sailors were running around and bumping into each other; some climbing up masts had to clamber over others trying to get down; one group was pulling on ropes to raise sails at the same time as another was struggling to lower them.

Even Sidney Smith joined in, crying, "*Dish out the milk rations and ready the fish as she goes!*" The only reason it didn't work was that there was no milk or fish on board. Captain Hazard tried to calm Sir Gadabout down – but once Sir Gadabout got as excited as this it was rather difficult to shut him up.

"*Avast the yardarms!*" he commanded. By now the sailors were in such a state of pandemonium that they didn't have time to try to work out what *that* one meant.

Sir Gadabout took a deep breath of sea air. "This is wonderful!" he said to Herbert. "I do believe I was born to go to sea."

But Herbert was not listening. Sir Gadabout's confusing orders were causing the *Flying Barnacle* to sail a crazy zigzag course out of the harbour and by now she was beginning to rock dangerously. Herbert was hanging over the side, feeling very seasick.

A cry of panic came from the lookout. "*We're heading for Jagger's Rocks!*"

Captain Hazard stopped trying to sort Sir Gadabout's mess out for a moment and rushed to look. He saw with dismay that they were indeed heading for some notorious rocks near the harbour mouth, and ran to the quarter-deck, yelling, "HARD A-STARBOARD!"

Sir Gadabout thought he ought to help out, too. "YES – AND HARD A-PORT, AS WELL!"

When Captain Hazard ordered all sails to be set so that they could turn quickly enough to take them away from the rocks, Sir Gadabout decided he couldn't see where they were going with all those sails flapping about and he ordered some of the bigger ones to be taken back in again.

The ship was still heading for the rocks and rocking wildly.

"W-we're k-kippered!" whimpered Sidney Smith, who hated getting wet.

"*I want to go home…*" groaned Herbert, still hanging over the side, looking green.

As the deadly Jagger's Rocks loomed up on the ship, Captain Hazard grabbed his charts and ran to the side to see if they were going to make it. Extra sailors threw their weight on the wheel, trying desperately to help the helmsmen turn the *Flying Barnacle* away from disaster.

At the very last second, the ship pulled away from the largest rocks and avoided being wrecked. However, she did glance off a small rock as she passed by. The jolt sent everyone flying – and Captain Hazard flying over the side into the sea.

"*MAN OVER!*" roared the lookout.

"We've got a man over?" said Sir Gadabout, thinking the lookout meant they had one man too many in the crew. "Can't have enough men when we face Longbeard – but that's jolly good counting from right up there."

Sidney Smith knew what the lookout meant. By now, Captain Hazard had hauled himself out of the water and on to the rocks. "Look, you pea brain!" said the angry cat. "Down there!"

"Ah," said Sir Gadabout, "Captain Hazard's decided to get off. Can't say I blame him –

he's not used to going into battle like I am. Never mind – full speed ahead, driver!"

As his ship and livelihood sailed into the distance, Captain Hazard waved his fists angrily. Sir Gadabout waved back. "Back in a jiffy! See you soon!"

"I see we've made our usual brilliant start," Sidney Smith observed, before slinking down below in search of rats and mice.

Sir Gadabout stood proudly on the quarterdeck, enjoying every moment of his first adventure at sea. But he had not noticed a ship appear on the horizon. The ship raised a black flag with a white skull and crossbones on it. Such a flag was known as the Jolly Roger – the pirates' flag.

3

Longbeard's Long-Gone Beard

The pirate ship waited in the distance to see which way the *Flying Barnacle* was going. But the *Flying Barnacle*, without her captain to guide her, had come to a halt and was going nowhere.

Sir Gadabout walked over to a couple of sailors who were standing by the mainmast. "Ahoy there, me friendies!" he greeted them.

"I think it's 'mateys', sire," said Herbert, who wasn't feeling so bad now that the ship had stopped moving.

Sir Gadabout didn't see the difference. "Now then, how do we get moving? Perhaps if we all get together and blow in the sails . . ."

One sailor shook his head. "No, sir – we've got the wind."

"Never mind," shrugged Sir Gadabout. "I

get it myself sometimes. We'll wait till you're feeling better, *then* we'll all blow in the sails."

"Sire, he means the wind blows the sails," said Herbert quietly.

"Er, of course! I knew *that*. Naturally." Sir Gadabout felt the wind in his hair and then looked at the limp sails. "So, why aren't we moving?"

"I think you've got to give the right orders, sir – tell the sailors which ropes to pull to make the sails catch the wind."

"Quite. So . . . what do I say?"

Eventually, they got the ship under way with the help of Little Jim, the quiet but helpful cabin boy, who seemed to be the only one around who knew which orders the captain normally gave.

Once the ship began ploughing through the waves again, Herbert turned as green as a carrot (that's accidentally fallen into a tin of green paint) and ran back to his "seasickness spot" at the ship's side.

Almost as soon as the *Flying Barnacle* was on the move, a cry came from the lookout that Longbeard's ship was heading their way.

"Oh, she is, is she? Well, he's never come up against Admiral Gadabout before! Right, me friendies, put lots of those heavy round things into the cannons and we'll show them who's boss! We'll rid these waters of the appalling pirates and get the wool to Chilliwilli."

"Cannonballs, sire," said Herbert. "That's what they put in." He had dragged himself away from the side – being more afraid of Longbeard than seasickness.

"Fine," agreed Sir Gadabout. "We'll add cannonballs if there's any room after the heavy round things have gone in. I've always wanted to see cannons being fired!"

"Sire, it *is* going to be very dangerous . . ." said Herbert.

"They'll never hit us from that far!"

"But they are closing on us fast. Those cannonballs can blast a hole in the side of the ship."

Sir Gadabout looked at the *Flying Barnacle*'s thick wooden walls and gave a little shudder. "Ah, well . . ."

Another voice said something, but nobody

heard it – so it tried again a little louder: "And then they'll try to jump on board our ship and finish us off with their daggers and cutlasses," warned Little Jim, the quiet cabin boy.

"They will?" gulped Sir Gadabout. "Well, er, I'm sure you can handle it. I've just remembered that I . . . forgot to feed my pet hamster. Got to go and find it – *quickly* before it starves to death!"

"You haven't *got* a pet hamster," Herbert pointed out as Sir Gadabout scampered away.

Longbeard's ship sped closer and closer, and there was a **BOOM!** like thunder as it fired its first broadside.

"*Eeek!*" Sir Gadabout whimpered, edging towards the hatchway that led below. "But – but what if *someone*'s got a pet hamster? And they've forgotten to feed it? It might die! Got to go!" With that, he scuttled down the steps like someone afraid for his life. (Which he was.)

Sir Gadabout spent quite a long time below. He thought he had better act naturally, so he crawled about on his hands and knees, calling, "*Here, Hammie! Where are you, Hammie?*"

The sailors getting the big guns on the

lower deck ready for firing stopped what they were doing and looked on in bewilderment as the knight crawled between their cannons.

"*Come to Daddy, Hammie! Has Longbeard gone yet? Where are you, little Hammie?*"

"It's just Sir Gadabout," Sidney Smith informed the sailors.

"Ah!" they said knowingly, and got on with their work.

But, strangely, there was no more firing from the pirates, no cries of battle from above. What in fact had happened was that Longbeard, realising that the *Flying Barnacle* was more or less helpless, decided to save his expensive cannonballs and offer the ship safe passage if they would hand over their cargo without a fight. The crew above deck had got together and decided it would be safer to accept his offer, and they started to pass the wool over to the *Nasty Piece of Work*, Longbeard's pirate ship. (Little Jim said he didn't agree, as it meant poor Captain Hazard would be ruined – but nobody heard him.)

Down below, Sir Gadabout was getting worried. Why was it all so quiet above? Eventually, he decided he had to find out. He stuck his head out of a porthole, and could see the pirates taking bales of wool on to their ship.

"Hey!" he shouted, unable to help himself. "That's *ours*!"

"That's Sir Gadalot – or something," called one of the pirates. "You know - the bloke who was chased by a little piggy!"

Sir Gadabout indignantly forced himself further out of the porthole to get a better look and tell them about the ferocious oink. But in doing so he had to clamber on to the cannon that was also sticking out of the porthole – a dangerous thing to do.

"NOOOOOO!" cried the man in charge of the cannon – but he was too late. Sir Gadabout's foot caught the firing mechanism, the gun went off and he was thrown into the air as it jerked backwards from the force of the explosion.

The cannonball shot upwards, took Longbeard's long beard clean off and singed his nose as it rose upwards and destroyed the Jolly Roger on its way into the sky.

"IT'S A TRAP, LADS!" cried the pirates, and immediately put the *Nasty Piece of Work* about and began to retreat.

The last thing anyone from the amazed crew of the *Flying Barnacle* heard was Longbeard vowing, "I'll get the lot of you, if it's the last thing I do!" as he rubbed his stubbly chin.

Sir Gadabout didn't hear any of this. He was lying on his back by the cannon, dazed

and deafened and with a bruised bottom. "Someone feed little Hammie when I'm gone . . ." he sighed weakly.

4

Once Sir Gadabout had come to his senses and gone up on deck, he was surprised to hear the crew cheering and crying things like *Hero*! and *Saved the day*! He looked behind him, thinking that someone else had arrived while he had been below – but no, they meant him!

Word had got round that the whole thing had been deliberately arranged by Sir Gadabout, who had personally fired the cannon that had taken off Longbeard's long beard.

"We're safe now Sir Gadabout's with us!" exclaimed a sailor.

"Haven't you heard about that little piggy . . ." Sidney Smith began – but Herbert put his hand over the cat's mouth.

"Oh, it was nothing!" said Sir Gadabout truthfully.

"But we had already handed over quite a lot of the precious wool," Little Jim pointed out quietly. But nobody heard him.

"Right, let's get going!" Sir Gadabout commanded.

But none of the crew moved. "Er – where to?" asked one salty seadog.

"Well – wherever you used to go with Captain Hazard . . ." Sir Gadabout replied.

"But the captain used to look at a map and work out which way to point the ship, sire."

"Captain Hazard had his charts with him when you knocked him overboard," Little Jim pointed out, but nobody heard him and they all rushed down to the captain's cabin to search for them.

Of course, they didn't find anything.

"Perhaps he took them with him when he decided to get off the boat," mused Sir Gadabout.

"*Ship*, sire," said Herbert.

"*Where*?" asked Sir Gadabout in a panicky voice. "Everybody hide under my table – I think there's room!"

"No, I mean they like you to call it a 'ship'. A boat's much smaller."

"Well, of course I knew that but I didn't think you would, that's all ... But what are we going to do about these maps?"

Herbert had a sudden brainwave. "What about our beachball? It's an inflatable globe!"

"Yes!" cried Sir Gadabout. "Let's go and play 'catch' instead – never mind about all this worrying sailing lark."

"He means a globe is like a map – only rounder, you lily-livered landlubber," said Sidney Smith, who had been hanging around with the ship's cat quite a lot.

They soon found the globe – but it took Sir Gadabout quite a bit longer to find the Chilliwilli islands.

"Ah!" cried Sir Gadabout finally. "There they are and it's not very far. About six centimetres!"

"It doesn't really work like that . . ." Little Jim warned them.

"But which way?" asked Herbert.

Sir Gadabout found England on the globe, traced a line to the Chilliwilli islands with his

finger and continued it out to sea through his cabin window. "That way!"

"Er, I don't think that's how you do it ..." said Little Jim. But nobody heard him.

Sidney Smith, who had much better hearing than humans, put a paw to his head and groaned.

"Start the engine and let's go!" declared Sir Gadabout.

The *Flying Barnacle* was on its way once more – but a dark ship flying a new black Jolly Roger was hovering in the distance, waiting. And on board was an angry, vengeful captain (wearing a false beard made out of an unfortunate sailor's hair – but pirates are mean like that).

5

Sir Gadabout to the Rescue

Thanks to Little Jim the quiet cabin boy running round the ship whispering the kind of orders he'd heard Captain Hazard give, the *Flying Barnacle* was soon sailing in good order. The only thing Little Jim didn't know about was navigation – how to work out which way to steer the ship. And Sir Gadabout's efforts with his beach ball globe weren't any help at all.

Once they had lost sight of land and could see only sea in every direction, it became almost impossible to know which way to go and they sailed aimlessly for quite some time while Sir Gadabout studied his beachball and gave a variety of nonsensical orders.

It kept him happy – until the lookout spotted the *Nasty Piece of Work* heading their way.

"They've crowded on all sail and are gaining on us!" the lookout yelled from above.

Sir Gadabout let out a fearful wail and began blowing into the nearest sail as hard as possible.

"I think you should give some orders, sire," said Herbert, who had overcome his sea-sickness by now and was actually quite enjoying life at sea. But Sir Gadabout had been blowing so much he had made himself dizzy, and was staggering about the quarterdeck with stars before his eyes.

Herbert decided to do his bit. "*Man the guns, lads!*" he cried, and sailors rushed from all parts of the ship to prepare the cannons above decks and below for firing.

"We're not fast enough. They're still catching us!" quailed Sir Gadabout after recovering from his dizziness. "Maybe if we get some men to go to the mast at the back and push?"

"And some to the mast at the front to pull?" suggested Sidney Smith sarcastically. When Sir Gadabout agreed, he groaned and scampered below before the cannonballs started flying.

Sir Gadabout stopped a passing sailor. "We need someone to push – go to the back," he ordered.

"*Stern*, sire," Herbert pointed out.

"Go to the back!" repeated Sir Gadabout sternly.

If only they could have put more sail on they could have kept ahead of the *Nasty Piece of Work*, but no one seemed to know where the extra sails were kept except Little Jim. He tried to tell them, but . . .

"Wool!" cried Herbert suddenly.

"Eh?" said Sir Gadabout, wondering whether worrying about the pirates had made his squire go mad.

"We can make sails of wool!"

And it worked. The crew hurriedly tied and stitched together enough fleeces to haul up as additional sails – and, gradually, the *Flying Barnacle* began to leave the pirate ship and its bloodthirsty crew behind. After a few hours they were nowhere to be seen.

The trouble was, the *Flying Barnacle* — as even Sir Gadabout now agreed — was completely lost.

They sailed for days without sight of land and when their supplies of food and water ran low, everyone began to worry.

Then Sir Gadabout scratched his head and found some tiny white flakes had fallen on to his shoulders. "*Eeek*!" he cried. "I've got scurvy!" (This caused a general panic among the crew, until it was explained that the little white flakes were *scurf*, or dandruff, and that scurvy was something a *lot* more unpleasant.)

To make matters worse, as the wind became stronger the woollen sails began to fall to pieces. If they didn't find land soon, the *Nasty Piece of Work* might find — and even catch up with — them. She couldn't be far away.

Just when the crew began to grumble that perhaps Sir Gadabout wasn't such a great captain after all, Little Jim the quiet cabin boy spotted something far away.

"Island!" he shouted in his loudest voice. "I can see an island!"

And, although nobody heard him, luckily

the lookout shouted, "ISLAND! I CAN SEE AN ISLAND!"

Sir Gadabout, Herbert and Sidney Smith ran to the side of the ship and stood beside Little Jim.

"That island looks familiar ..." said Little Jim.

"At last, I've reached my first far-flung, distant land!" cried Sir Gadabout excitedly.

"Er ... It looks like the Isle of Wight, sir," said Little Jim.

"Maybe I'm the first man to discover it. I could become famous!"

"It's *definitely* the Isle of Wight ..."

"Well done, sire!" said Herbert. "I hereby name this newly discovered island *Gadabout Land*!"

Sir Gadabout put his telescope to his eye. "But wait – there are natives on the beach! They look angry. They seem to be chasing two innocent people into the sea. I should

43

imagine they're cannibals after a meal! TO THE RESCUE! LOWER THE BOATS! GET THE STRONGEST ROWERS!"

"It's only the Isle of Wight!" Little Jim repeated. But nobody heard him.

6
Well, Sort of . . .

King Arthur, the head of the Knights of the Round Table, was paddling in the sea. But he didn't go too deep and he was on the lookout for jellyfish – he was frightened of jellyfish.

Guinevere, his beautiful queen, was also paddling. But she wasn't worried about jellyfish. She was trying out the prototype desalination plant she had built out of driftwood, seashells and other stuff she'd found on the beach.

They always came to the Isle of Wight for their holidays. King Arthur loved the amusement arcades and Queen Guinevere – when she wasn't building desalination plants – was working on a new invention. It was a long wooden walkway that took you out over the sea. She thought she might call it a 'pier' when it was finished.

The mayor and all the other important people also loved it when the illustrious King Arthur and Queen Guinevere came to the Isle of Wight. It made their little island famous and popular – and they could proudly put up *By Royal Appointment* signs everywhere.

That was why wherever the king and queen went, the mayor and his official party followed them. Whenever King Arthur jumped over a little wave, the mayor and his company clapped and cheered. Whenever Queen Guinevere produced another litre of desalinated water, they cried, "*Bravo!*" politely.

The king and queen loved their little holidays of peace and quiet (apart from the mayor and his party) on the Isle of Wight. That was . . . until they looked up and saw two boat-

loads of tough-looking, armed men rowing furiously towards them. At the front of the leading boat a spindly knight stood waving his sword and shouting warlike things – until he fell into the sea and had to be pulled out glugging and gurgling.

"Isn't that . . ." began King Arthur with dismay.

"It *couldn't* be . . ." groaned Queen Guinevere.

7

Sir Gadabout Runs Away

"I'll save you from the cannibals!" shouted Sir Gadabout. Actually, his mouth was still full of water and seaweed and it came out as, "*Gloopily-bubble-bluuurgh - hic!*"

"It must be some kind of battle re-enactment the king and queen have laid on for us," said the mayor, applauding enthusiastically.

"HURRAH!" cried his important guests.

"Hurry!" yelled Sir Gadabout. "Those cannibals are getting restless!"

"Isn't that the king and queen they're chasing?" asked Herbert.

"My word, you're right, Herbert! Row quicker, men – we can't have the king and queen being eaten by cannibals!"

"*Especially* not the queen," added Herbert – who secretly thought she was extremely beautiful.

"Now, now – they're both equally royal," Sir Gadabout pointed out in fairness. "But – yes, especially the queen." (He secretly fancied her, too.)

"Jolly good show!" said the mayor as Sir Gadabout and his men jumped out of their boats and waded ashore with blood-curdling cries and swords brandished above their heads.

As they approached the king and queen, King Arthur said to the mayor, "Allow me to introduce you to one of my knights, Sir Gad—"

But Sir Gadabout led his men right past the king, crying, "Into them, men!"

"Oh, dear . . ." groaned King Arthur.

The mayor and his party suddenly realised that the invaders meant business and they all turned and fled.

"Er . . . I believe there may have been some kind of . . ." began King Arthur. But his words were drowned out by Sir Gadabout shouting, "ATTACK! ATTACK!" as he chased after the mayor and his dignitaries in the direction of Ventnor.

King Arthur stood staring forlornly at the trail of footprints in the sand, then sat down and buried his head in his hands. "Good grief . . ."

"At least he looked kind of . . . *brave,*" Guinevere commented.

"Yes," agreed the king. "I suppose for once he did look—" But King Arthur's words were drowned out by Sir Gadabout again.

He and his men were being chased by the mayor's constables and the enraged citizens of the Isle of Wight. As he hurtled back to the boats, crying, "RETREAT! RETREAT!" Sir Gadabout accidentally knocked the king into a hole in the sand that the king had been working on all morning.

"Good grief . . ." came a voice from the hole.

8

The Final Showdown

"The *mayor*?" gasped Sir Gadabout.

"Yes, you blundering buffoon!" said Sidney Smith. They were back on board the ship.

"But, you mean, I . . . you mean, the king – and queen – and the *mayor* – and all those important people . . ."

"Yes, you dithering dunderhead! I saw it all through Little Jim's telescope!"

"Oh dear," gulped Sir Gadabout. "Er, do you think the king noticed me?"

"He probably thought you were some kind of pirate, sire," suggested Herbert.

Sir Gadabout cheered up. "Yes – that's it! Some kind of pirate!"

"Some kind of nutcase, more like," muttered Sidney Smith, sloping off to gossip about it with the ship's cat.

They left the Isle of Wight rather

hurriedly and, once again, Sir Gadabout studied his beachball globe in order to decide the direction of the Chilliwilli islands.

"You can't navigate like that!" cried an exasperated Sidney Smith, who had rejoined them.

"This is a very accurate beachball – the man at the shop told me so!" said Sir Gadabout.

"*And* it's got pictures of whales and dolphins," added Herbert.

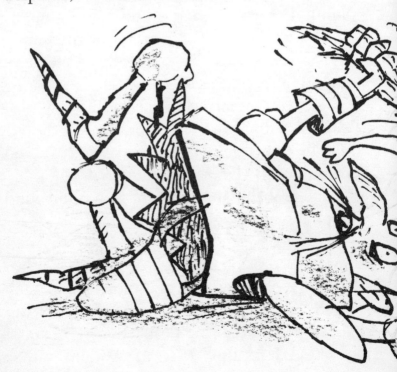

"But if you don't know where you are and you don't know where north, south, east and west are, it's blinking *useless*," argued Sidney Smith.

"Ah, but I do know where I am – on board the *Flying Barnacle*!" Sir Gadabout declared decisively.

"Oh, give the stupid thing to me!" said Sidney Smith trying to grab it off him.

"I'm the captain!" cried Sir Gadabout.

As they wrestled for the beachball, Sidney

Smith's sharp claws caught it. There was a loud hissing noise and it began to slowly shrink and shrivel. Sir Gadabout desperately tried to stop the hole with his finger.

"Now look what you've done," said Sidney Smith. "You've made a hole in the sea – all the water will drain away and we'll be stranded."

"Aargh! Will we?" gasped Sir Gadabout, rushing to a porthole to look outside. The sea still looked pretty deep to him – but the beachball had completely deflated and was now just a crumpled, wrinkly piece of plastic.

"Very clever!" Herbert scolded the cat. "*Now* how are we going to know which way to go?"

As it happened, it didn't really matter, for during the cloudy, moonless night a dark ship crept quietly and steadily closer. Its cannons were fully loaded, its crew patiently watched the lanterns of the *Flying Barnacle* to make sure she did not escape this time. Its captain waited silently with pistols and cutlass (and false beard) for his revenge.

When daylight came, the crew of the *Flying Barnacle* discovered the terrible truth: the *Nasty Piece of Work* was right alongside them, with all guns loaded and ready to fire. They were so close that the pirates' broadside would undoubtedly sink their ship.

Sir Gadabout was sent for – but he proved difficult to rouse from his sleep. He was dreaming about rescuing Queen Guinevere from wild cannibals wearing mayors' chains of office. She was so impressed by Sir Gadabout's heroics that she asked him to marry her. King Arthur thought this was only fair (well, it *was* a dream) and they had just got to the part where the vicar asks Sir Gadabout if he takes Guinevere to be his lawful wedded wife, when . . .

"*Wake up, sire! Don't you know there's a pirate ship alongside?*" asked Herbert.

"I do! I do!" cried Sir Gadabout, still not really awake.

"I think it's all over, sire!"

"I know — time for our kiss!" Sir Gadabout held out his arms and puckered his lips. Herbert realised that his master was still dreaming and gave him an urgent shake to wake him up.

Sir Gadabout dreamed that it was King Arthur trying to prevent the marriage and he ended up wrestling with Herbert, shouting, "*You're too late! It's me she loves!*" Some of the crew who had come to see what the matter was stood looking on in wonderment. (They weren't used to Sir Gadabout.)

Eventually it all got sorted out and Sir Gadabout rushed up on deck. There, he was confronted by the sight of the powerful pirate ship with all guns bristling – and Longbeard at the rails, calling to him.

"Finally we meet, Sir Gadalot!" growled the pirate captain. "You are defeated! Hand over your cargo and all other valuables and then I shall take my painful revenge for the time you shot my . . ." he put a hand to his false beard made from a sailor's hair, " . . . *almost* shot my beard off. As you can see, it's still intact, but, er, it was a close thing."

"You might say it was a close *shave*!" chortled Sidney Smith.

Some of Longbeard's own crew sniggered at this (especially the man who'd had his hair chopped off to make the beard), but they were soon silenced by an evil glance from their captain – the most feared pirate between Land's End and the Isle of Wight.

"You have until noon to hand over everything, Sir Gadalot!"

"-*ABOUT*!" Sir Gadabout corrected him.

"All right, you've got till *about* noon – or I sink the *Flying Barnacle* and everyone in it!"

And he laughed so evilly and so much that his beard began to slip so he had to stop. But they'd got the message.

"What shall we do, sire?" asked Herbert.

"We – we could hide down below," Sir Gadabout suggested. "I've seen some big barrels that we might be able to get into and—"

"That'll be a lot of use when the ship's sinking," snorted Sidney Smith.

Sir Gadabout looked hopefully over the

side. "I don't suppose the sea's drained down the hole yet?"

Meanwhile, Longbeard and his crew counted the minutes till they could blow the *Flying Barnacle* out of the water . . .

9

Sir Gadabout Walks the Plank

Little Jim the quiet cabin boy had a plan.

Naturally, no one noticed at first but, when he wrote it down for them, it all began to make sense. The *Nasty Piece of Work* had far bigger and better guns than the *Flying Barnacle* (not to mention more of them), so a fight was out of the question. Little Jim decided the only answer was to turn their own guns on *themselves*. They would surrender to the pirates and let them come on board. Then, while the pirates were busy plundering, the *Flying Barnacle* crew could sneak across to the pirate ship and take over *her* guns!

"It just might work," said Herbert.

"Yes," remarked Sidney Smith glumly. "We could risk our necks for a load of old wool and try to trick a mob of cut-throat pirates who would chop us to pieces and eat our innards for the price of a pint. Or we could just give them the load of old wool."

"*Never!*" Sir Gadabout declared. "Er . . . what was that plan again? We go there, then they come here, then we come back here, but first they go . . ."

They left Sir Gadabout trying to figure it all out and rushed up on deck to contact Longbeard and pretend to surrender.

Longbeard and most of his crew came across in boats, laughing and cheering at what they thought was their easy victory. But Sidney Smith pointed out that they had left a few men on board the *Nasty Piece of Work* to guard it.

"Never mind about them," said Herbert, smacking one of his big fists into the palm of his other hand. "We can take care of *them*!"

Once on board, Longbeard strode up to Sir Gadabout. He was tall and lean, with a black patch over one eye and a large ugly scar on his cheek. He was stroking his false beard angrily, and his dark little eye pierced Sir Gadabout like a laser beam.

Sir Gadabout tried to run below. "I forgot to fold my pyjamas neatly!" he cried. But his way was barred by burly pirates.

"If it isn't Sir Gadalot!" hissed Longbeard.

"V–very pleased to meet you," replied Sir Gadabout, hoping that Longbeard was going to be civilised after all. He held out his hand to shake – but quickly pulled it back to avoid Longbeard's sword as it swished down viciously.

"This is the man who shot – er, *nearly* shot – my magnificent, long beard off. But I was too quick for him, wasn't I, boys?"

"Yes, boss!" cried his men loyally (except a shaven-headed pirate, who just mumbled something under his breath).

"And you know what we do to people who nearly shoot a pirate's magnificent long beard off, don't you, boys?"

"Er – let them go home if they say sorry?" wondered Sir Gadabout.

But the pirates ignored him and began to roar, "*PLANK! PLANK! PLANK!*"

"We make him *walk the plank*," said Longbeard with glee. "Set it up, boys!"

Three sailors began to fix a long plank so that it stuck out over the side of the ship.

"So ..." began Sir Gadabout, "I have to walk to the end and back again? But what if I fall in? I must say, it looks rather wobbly ..."

"Falling in is the idea," laughed Longbeard cruelly.

"But you don't understand – I can't swim!"

"Even better," Longbeard sneered. He turned to his men. "While I'm making him walk the plank at the point of my sword, you lot go and get the wool. We'll make *thousands* when we get it to the Chilliwilli islands!"

Now, Little Jim put the first part of his idea into operation. "Oh, dear," he yelled. (He was  using a speaking trumpet – a sort of loud hailer – so that they could all hear him.) "I hope they don't find the captain's stock of fine wines and brandy!"

Sailors – especially pirates – can't resist booze of any kind (so it's said) and the pirates immediately stampeded down to the lower decks in search of poor Captain Hazard's supply of wine and brandy – and wool, of course.

Little Jim winked at Herbert. He knew the pirates would be dead drunk in no time at all.

Meantime, Sir Gadabout, prodded by Longbeard's sword, put one foot on to the plank – which felt very shaky. "I wonder if I could have a life jacket or something?" Sir Gadabout suggested. One look into Longbeard's evil eye told him the answer.

Sir Gadabout knew that there was a plan – something about them coming here and us going there and them going back there . . . Why wasn't something happening to save his life?

"So this is your **PLAN**!" shouted Sir Gadabout. He hoped his men – who didn't seem to be doing very much – would get the message. "I see you **PLAN** to let me fall in the sea and ruin my **PLAN** to save the wool!" Still nobody moved to put the **PLAN** – sorry, plan – into action. He did not realise that they could only wait for Longbeard's crew to get blind drunk.

"Enough of your *plans*," snarled Longbeard, and he pushed Sir Gadabout further along the plank with the point of his sword.

"**PLANS**?" said Sir Gadabout, waving his

arms around to try to keep his balance. He felt sure he saw a shark circling below. "Did I mention **PLAN**? I don't remember even using the word **PLAN**!" As he shouted the word he looked imploringly at his crew – but still they didn't budge.

"*Move!*" Longbeard pushed Sir Gadabout almost to the end of the plank.

Sir Gadabout looked down at the waves below and let out a pitiful wail. "**PLAN! PLAN! PLAN!**" he screamed repeatedly.

"I'd heard he was mad – looks like it's true,"

said Longbeard to himself.

Sir Gadabout continued shouting and, in his panic, began stamping his feet on the plank. The plank began to bounce like a swimming pool diving board and, before he knew it, Sir Gadabout was flying up into the air. His belt caught on the end of a yardarm – one of the long poles that the sails are attached to – and he was left dangling in the air with his legs and arms flailing wildly.

"You won't get away from me that easily," Longbeard cursed. He put his dagger between his teeth and began to climb up the mast.

Meantime, Herbert sneaked quietly down below. He spied the pirates swigging everything they could lay their hands on. They were roaring drunk, sprawled all over the place, singing and laughing.

Herbert rushed back on deck. "It's worked. Let's go!"

They all swarmed into the pirates' boats and rowed across to the *Nasty Piece of Work*, where they easily overpowered the few pirates left in charge of her. Then they manned the guns pointing at the *Flying Barnacle*.

Just then, Sir Gadabout's belt snapped. He plummeted seaward with a screech like a walrus with a sore throat – but, instead of falling into the water, he landed on the plank, bounced back into the air and landed in Herbert's arms on board the pirate ship.

"Was this the plan?" he asked his squire groggily.

"Er, *sort of*, sire," replied Herbert.

Longbeard climbed back down the mast and began cursing them. "You'll all pay for this! I'll feed you to the sharks! I'll . . . " He heard the drunken singing of his men coming from below (not to mention some snoring). "I'll . . ." He saw his own mighty guns all pointing straight at him. His look of hatred turned instantly into a smarmy smile. "Gentlemen – perhaps we can come to some sort of agreement . . ."

10

Sir Gadabout Pulls the Plug

Sir Gadabout leaned over the side of the *Nasty Piece of Work* and called to Longbeard. "Now listen carefully, my good fellow! I want you to throw all your weapons over the side and —"

"What?" cried Longbeard, putting a hand to his ear.

"What?" asked Sir Gadabout.

"He can't hear you," explained Little Jim. But Sir Gadabout couldn't hear him.

"I said, LISTEN CAREFULLY!"

"What?" shouted Longbeard.

"Right!" said Sir Gadabout, and he began to climb on to a cannon so that he could lean further out over the side of the ship.

"I don't think that's a good idea ..." Little Jim warned him.

Sir Gadabout scrambled along the barrel of the cannon.

"Please watch where you put your feet ..."

There was a loud **BOOOOM** and a puff
of black smoke. Sir Gadabout was thrown
back into Herbert's arms.

"My word, these ships are dangerous
places . . ." gasped Sir Gadabout dizzily.

The cannonball smashed into the side of
the *Flying Barnacle*, just above the waterline,
and the ship's crew watched in dismay as
water began to pour through the hole.

They could hear Longbeard summoning
his men and shouting that they were under

attack and sinking. The pirates who could still walk helped those who couldn't and they launched the *Flying Barnacle*'s own boats and began rowing away as fast as they could before any more cannonballs came their way.

"Good shot, sire!" cheered Herbert.

"But poor Captain Hazard's ship – and all his wool!" groaned Sir Gadabout as he watched the water gushing in through the hole.

"I've got an idea," Herbert exclaimed – and promptly dived over the side and swam

towards the *Flying Barnacle*. Once there, he hauled himself through the jagged hole, gasping and spluttering, and disappeared inside the ship. Very soon, large bails of wool began to appear in the hole – until finally it was completely plugged and the ship was no longer sinking.

"Brilliant!" said Sir Gadabout.

"There won't be much wool left at this rate . . ." Little Jim warned. But nobody heard him.

The weather turned very cold on the journey home (they made their way by stopping along the coast every few miles and asking for directions – but they decided to miss out the Isle of Wight), so they ingeniously made cloaks of wool to keep themselves warm. And yet more wool was used up because they had to keep replacing the plug in the hole.

Finally, they sailed back into the *Flying Barnacle*'s home port. A cheering crowd awaited them, since news of their arrival had quickly spread along the coast from all the places they had stopped at. The Donkey Man was there and the ice-cream seller – even King Arthur and Queen Guinevere were there (since their holiday had been ruined they were on their way back to Camelot at the time). Most importantly of all, Captain Hazard was there, waiting to see his ship come safely home.

"So, Longbeard shot a hole in my ship, I see!" said Captain Hazard, who nevertheless greeted them warmly.

"Er . . ." began Herbert, not quite sure how to put it.

"It was Gadabout!" said Sidney Smith – who was.

"Oh, well, never mind. And I hear a little of the wool has gone – stolen by Longbeard?" asked Captain Hazard, beginning to look less cheerful.

"Er . . ." began Herbert.

"Gadabout used it – surprising how many things you can do with wool!" said Sidney Smith.

Captain Hazard noticed that most of his crew wore woollen cloaks. "I see . . . Well, at least I still have my beautiful ship!"

"And not *all* the wool has gone!" cried Sir Gadabout. He bounded back into the ship.

"You don't think he's actually going to . . ." said Captain Hazard, who seemed close to tears by now.

The wool that was plugging the hole began to wiggle and waggle.

"He wouldn't – would he?" Arthur asked Guinevere quietly.

The wool began to move more violently.

"*He's actually going to do it . . .*" sobbed Captain Hazard.

"He's Sir *Gadabout*!" explained Sidney Smith.

The wool popped out. The water flooded in. The *Flying Barnacle* glugged lower and lower, and then was gone for good.

Seconds later, Sir Gadabout rose majestically out of the water like a surfacing dolphin. He had lost most of the wool in struggling to the surface and doggy-paddling to the quayside, though he still clutched a piece about the size of a handkerchief, which he waved triumphantly over his head.

"*Success!*"

Captain Hazard had to be led away to lie down in a darkened room. He was not himself for many days – but was soon back in good spirits when King Arthur decided it was only fair to repay the captain everything he had lost and Guinevere built him a brand new ship which was so fast and so strong that no pirate would ever be able to trouble him again. Captain Hazard named it the *Guinevere* in her honour (despite the fact that the crew wanted to call it the *Gadabout Never Again*).

Due to the terrible effects of the cannon-ball, Longbeard was never able to grow his long beard again. He was last heard of recovering in Dr Addlehead's Home for Befuddled Pirates. He is said to shout and throw things around whenever other patients try to shave in the morning and he spends most of his time making little models of knights in armour and then hitting them with a hammer, giggling, "Got you now! Got you now!" Some of his old crew visit him from time to time – but they've learned *never* to wear woollen clothes.

"You should have seen me plug the hole in the *Flying Barnacle*," Herbert told anyone who would listen back at Camelot. "It takes more strength than you'd think to shove wool into a hole when the sea's trying to get in, let me tell you."

"I had to lie along the barrel of the gun to make sure it was lined up to get Longbeard's beard . . ." Sir Gadabout explained. "It was dangerous – but worth it in the end."

"Just being in the same place as Gadabout for five minutes is dangerous," said Sidney

Smith. "But whether it's worth it in the end . . . that's another story."

And, although everyone knew deep down that Sir Gadabout was still the Worst Knight in the World (except now they knew it applied to both land *and* sea), it was quite a while before they mentioned it again.

Also by Martyn Beardsley

Sir Gadabout

When the fair Guinevere goes missing, Sir Gadabout sets out to rescue her . . . and he's in for some catastrophic adventures!

Sir Gadabout Gets Worse

When Excalibur is stolen, Sir Gadabout sets off with his trusty band of followers to find the evil Sir Rudyard the Rancid. They must face the worst if they are to return the mighty sword to its rightful home.

Sir Gadabout and The Ghost

When he sees the ghost of Sir Henry
Hirsute, Sir Gadabout runs up the wall in
fright. But soon he's off on another
calamitous quest – to clear Sir Henry's
name of the ghastly crime of pilchard
stealing.

Sir Gadabout Does His Best

Take a three legged goat, a hungry dragon and a bad tempered, short knight called Sir Mistabit. Mix well with Sir Gadabout, the worst knight in the world, and his trusty companions.

What have you got? A recipe for disaster as Sir Gadabout and Co set off on a chaotic and hilarious, brand new adventure.

Sir Gadabout and the Little Horror

He looks like an angel, but he's a little horror called Roger and he causes chaos in Camelot as he runs rings around Sir Gadabout and Co with his dire and dastardly deeds.

The Worst Knight in the World is no match for this small boy . . . or is he? Read on and discover whether Sir Gadabout outwits wicked Roger in this hilarious adventure.